Dear Parents,

W9-CNU-451

Welcome to the Scholastic Reader series. We have taken over 80 years of experience with teachers, parents, and children and put it into a program that is designed to match your child's interests and skills.

Level 1— Short sentences and stories made up of words kids can sound out using their phonics skills and words that are important to remember.

Level 2— Longer sentences and stories with words kids need to know and new "big" words that they will want to know.

Level 3— From sentences to paragraphs to longer stories, these books have large "chunks" of texts and are made up of a rich vocabulary.

Level 4— First chapter books with more words and fewer pictures.

It is important that children learn to read well enough to succeed in school and beyond. Here are ideas for reading this book with your child:

- Look at the book together. Encourage your child to read the title and make a prediction about the story.
- Read the book together. Encourage your child to sound out words when appropriate. When your child struggles, you can help by providing the word.
- Encourage your child to retell the story. This is a great way to check for comprehension.
- Have your child take the fluency test on the last page to check progress.

Scholastic Readers are designed to support your child's efforts to learn how to read at every age and every stage. Enjoy helping your child learn to read and love to read.

　　　　—Francie Alexander
　　　　Chief Education Officer
　　　　Scholastic Education

For Isobel Louise — welcome
R.I.

To Kath
K.M.

No part of this publication may be reproduced, or stored in a retrieval system, or transmitted in any form or by any means, electronic, mechanical, photocopying, recording, or otherwise, without written permission of the publisher. For information regarding permission, write to Scholastic Inc., Attention: Permissions Department, 557 Broadway, New York, NY 10012.

Text copyright © 2003 by Rose Impey.
Illustrations copyright © 2003 by Katharine McEwen.
Originally published in Great Britain under the title *Titchy Witch and the Bully Boggarts*.

Library of Congress Cataloging-in-Publication Data available.

Published by Scholastic Inc.
SCHOLASTIC, CARTWHEEL BOOKS, and associated logos are trademarks and/or registered trademarks of Scholastic Inc.

ISBN 0-439-73000-7

10 9 8 7 6 5 4 3 2   05 06 07 08 09

Printed in the U.S.A.   23
This edition first printing, August 2005

Wanda Witch
and the Bullies

Rose Impey ★ Katharine McEwen

Scholastic Reader — Level 3

Cartwheel
·B·O·O·K·S·®

SCHOLASTIC INC.

New York   Toronto   London   Auckland   Sydney
Mexico City   New Delhi   Hong Kong   Buenos Aires

Wanda Witch

Victor

Eric

Wendel

Weeny Witch

Witchy Witch

Cat-a-bogus

Wanda Witch didn't want to go to school. She said she had a tummy-ache.

"Too many Grobble Gums," said Cat-a-bogus.

"All little witches have to go to school," said Mom.

"Even this little witch," said Dad.

Wanda Witch wanted Mom to
take her to school, but Witchy Witch
was too busy with the baby.

So Cat-a-bogus took her instead.
Wanda Witch was not happy.

She didn't want anyone to see her
being taken to school by a cat!
But Gobby Gool saw her.

When Wanda Witch stuck her
nose in the air, Gobby tripped her.

So Wanda Witch turned his nose
into a hot dog.

I'll tell
my brother
on you!

It soon turned back, but Gobby
was still mad.

Gobby Gool's brother was a
terrible bully.
He stood on Wanda Witch's foot
and twisted her arm behind
her back.

So she turned his head into
a cabbage!

"You wait," said the cabbage.
"After school, our cousins will get
you! They're goblins!"

But Wanda Witch didn't even wait
for Cat-a-bogus.
She started walking home on her own.

When Wanda Witch was
halfway home, she heard a
whis-whis-whispering sound.

She knew what it was.
You could smell goblins
a mile away.

Seven of them jumped out of the bushes. (Goblins always travel in groups.)

Wanda Witch wasn't afraid of one goblin. But seven?!

The goblins called her names.

They pulled her hair and pinched
her hat.

They tried to make Wanda Witch
cry, but even little witches
never cry.

"My dad will turn you all into toads," she said bravely.

"Let him," croaked the goblins.

"My mom will turn you all into pigs," she said.

"Who cares?" grunted the goblins.

Then Wanda Witch had
a great idea.
She made up a spell:

"Pinch of sugar, pinch of spice.
All things pink and sweet and nice.
Turn these goblins, brown and hairy,
Into little goblin-fairies."

The goblins stared at one another
and started to squeal.

When they saw Cat-a-bogus
coming, the goblin-fairies
ran away.

Cat-a-bogus told Wanda Witch she was getting too big for her broomstick.

He made her promise she would always wait for him from now on.

Cat-a-bogus was glad she'd learned her lesson for once.

But Wanda Witch was planning
a little lesson of her own.

Fluency Fun

The words in each list below end in the same sounds.
Read the words in a list.
Read them again.
Read them faster.
Try to read all 15 words in one minute.

way	mice	itch
gray	nice	pitch
play	rice	witch
stay	price	twitch
away	spice	stitch

Look for these words in the story.

busy	instead	brother
head	idea	

Note to Parents:
According to *A Dictionary of Reading and Related Terms*, fluency is "the ability to read smoothly, easily, and readily with freedom from word-recognition problems." Fluency is necessary for good comprehension and enjoyable reading. The activities on this page include a speed drill and a sight-recognition drill. Speed drills build fluency because they help students rapidly recognize common syllables and spelling patterns in words, and they're fun! Sight-recognition drills help students smoothly and accurately recognize words. Practice these activities with your child to help him or her become a fluent reader.
—**Wiley Blevins**,
Reading Specialist